The Ocean Between Us

Written by

Rhonda H. Bishop

Illustrated by

Cass Barth

Rhonda H. Bishop

AuthorHouse™ UK Ltd.
500 Avebury Boulevard
Central Milton Keynes, MK9 2BE
www.authorhouse.co.uk
Phone: 08001974150

First published by AuthorHouse 9/30/2008

ISBN: 978-1-4389-0448-1 (sc)

Library of Congress Control Number: 2008906868

Printed in the United States of America
Bloomington, Indiana

This book is printed on acid-free paper.

authorHOUSE®

DEDICATION

To the courage of the military child.

ACKNOWLEDGEMENTS by Rhonda H. Bishop

I would like to acknowledge and give thanks to Linda Brown, high school English teacher, for editing this book and also for her kind words of praise.

I am also indebted to my lifelong friend, and English professor, Nancy Mack. Not only did she give me her personal opinion but her professional one as well. It was at that time that I began to believe that the story of Sophia would be widely accepted.

I will be forever grateful to my dear friend and sorority sister, Cass Barth for making Sophia come to life with her beautiful illustrations. She has drawn the love and warmth that I hope my words will be able to convey to all who read this book.

ACKNOWLEDGEMENTS by Cass Barth

Thank you Alexandra for your willingness to be Sophia, Luke, Sophia's cousin, and Bob, Sophia's grandpa. And to Zachary and Kadelyn who watched as their siblings brought, "The Ocean Between Us" to life.

My name is Sophia and I love to play in the sand. I used to play in the sand table at the daycare and the sand box at the park, and now I can play at the beach.

Mommy and I just moved to Virginia where Grandma and Grandpa live in a small house close to the ocean.

The water was the same color as my favorite sweater, and it mixes with the sand to build the very best sand castles. At bedtime the waves roll in to wash them away and smooth out the beach for a new day of play.

When we moved to Virginia, Mommy took me out to the beach and told me that soon she would have to leave to take a trip to the other side of this ocean to a place called Iraq. Iraq would have lots of sand too. While she was gone, it would be my job to make Grandma and Grandpa smile.

My job will be a lot easier than my Mommy's. There are many people who need Mommy's help. Some of them are soldiers and some are children just like me. She is a doctor with super hero band-aids for wherever it might hurt. I think the soldiers will like that a lot.

My mommy knows how much I will miss her while she is gone, so she gave me a pretty blue jar with gummi bears inside. She told me if I ate just one bear each day while she was gone, by the time the jar was empty she would be back at Grandma and Grandpa's house to play with me in the sand. I think I will trick Mommy and eat all of the bears really fast so she will get to come home even sooner. Silly Mommy! Why didn't she think of that?

Before my mommy left to go to Iraq we had a great big picnic at the beach. There were aunts and uncles and so many cousins I couldn't even count them all. I feel sorry for people who don't have cousins because cousins are a lot of fun. I gave a great big bear hug like Grandpa always gives me to every cousin. Those hugs always make me feel special.

Grandpa told us stories about our moms and dads when they were little and how they would go down to the beach and dig a tunnel under the sand. It would go all the way out to the ocean. Maybe I could dig one that would take me to my mommy when she goes to Iraq. If I could do that, then there would be no ocean between us any more. I could see her whenever I wanted. I will talk to Grandpa about this idea later.

On the last day before Mommy left, we showed Grandma and Grandpa how to make cookies from play dough with Grandma's collection of cookie cutters. You can't really eat them, but they sure did make them smile. I think I am going to be good at this job of making Grandma and Grandpa smile.

One day after Mommy left, the letter carrier brought a package with my name on it to the house. Mommy had sent me a special present that made me smile. When I opened it, there was a box inside full of sand that had come all the way from Iraq. There was also a note from Mommy. "Sophia dear," it said, "Here is the sand I see every day where I work. Sometimes I even get to see the ocean. There is an ocean of love that fills my heart when I think about you being so happy while living with Grandma and Grandpa."

Now when I look at the ocean, I can see that it is the same ocean Mommy looks at when she thinks of me. And when I look up into the heavens where God is watching over all of us, I know Mommy will be just fine and come home soon to play again with me in the sand.

RHONDA H. BISHOP, AUTHOR
BIOGRAPHY

Rhonda H. Bishop has worked with young children for more than 20 years. It was just three years ago that she began working with young children of military families at Wright Patterson Air Force Base in Ohio. It has been a life changing experience which lead to the writing of "The Ocean Between Us." This is her first book.

CASS BARTH, ILLUSTRATOR
BIOGRAPHY

Cass Barth has dabbled in the arts all of her years as an elementary teacher. Retirement has allowed her to become a serious artist. Her illustrations for "Ocean Between Us" are colored pencil on saturated cardstock.

Printed in the United States
127286LV00002B